Evacuation

Praise for *Saving Mozart*

'This slender, confident debut novel is deliciously atmospheric and tense.' *Financial Times*

'A dazzling, striking novel, as intriguing as its author... An unconditional success.' *L'Express*

'The deceptively simple story of an improbable hero is a parable of personal bravery, ethics and responsibility...A petite gem.' *Weekend Press*

'Suspenseful and moving.' *North & South*

'The author's own love and understanding of music shines through every page. Jerusalmy has produced a perfectly crafted addition to the best of Holocaust literature.' *Daily Mail*

'It reads like an unexpected gift...This is a novel that will astonish and delight. I found it hugely moving, not least because of the overwhelming sense of loss, of a life that is spent, of the material objects that we gather around us ultimately being meaningless.' *Big Issue* UK

'An ingenious reinvention of the Holocaust narrative.' *Australian Financial Review*

'Nothing can detract from the sheer genius of the plot and the dazzling display of heroism which is at the core of this absolute gem of a novel.' *Weekend Bookworm*

'Jewel-like.' *Sydney Morning Herald*

'An immensely powerful book told with economy and heart.' *Bait for Bookworms*

Praise for *Evacuation*

'Raphaël Jerusalmy's new novel is without a doubt his best...
It transports you to a life in which readers must make choices,
or at least wonder what choice they would make in this
situation. A novel worthy of the best in suspense literature.
This is fiction from which each reader will draw life lessons.
A highly original novel.' *Page des libraires*

'Although the Israeli Arab conflict is the background to his
novel, Raphaël Jerusalmy broadens the scope in a spectacular
way...He weaves a tale of heartrending universality.
Rather than shrugging off history, he confronts it in
his own superbly literary way.' *L'Humanité*

'In this marvellous book, Raphaël Jerusalmy shows us that,
despite the destructive madness of men, a few beautiful
spirits, angel-poets, will always remain.' *Le Monde*

'By combining truth and the untruth, certainty and
uncertainty, Raphaël Jerusalmy manages easily, such
is his huge talent, to transport us to the other side of a
mirror, which is less distorting than it appears...Magic
is not something imaginary; you just have to forget
the walls and they'll come down and make way for
dreams, good or bad.' *Sud-Ouest*

'Enchanting, poetic and perceptive.' *L'Express*

'A brilliant, cinematographic, Middle Eastern
road movie of a novel.' *Le Monde des livres*

'An urban ode to the desire to live, and to peace.'
Biblioteca Magazine

Raphaël Jerusalmy holds degrees from the École Normale Supérieure and the Sorbonne. He made his career in the Israeli military intelligence services before working in the humanitarian and educational fields. He is now a novelist and antiquarian book dealer in Tel Aviv. His first novel, *Saving Mozart*, is also published by Text.

Penny Hueston has translated novels by Marie Darrieussecq, Patrick Modiano and Sarah Cohen-Scali.

RAPHAËL JERUSALMY
Evacuation

Translated from the French by Penny Hueston

TEXT PUBLISHING MELBOURNE AUSTRALIA

textpublishing.com.au

The Text Publishing Company
Swann House
22 William Street
Melbourne Victoria 3000
Australia

First published as *Evacuation* by Actes Sud, 2017
First published in English by The Text Publishing Company, 2018

Cover design by Actes Sud
Cover photograph by J.D.S. / Shutterstock
Text design by Jessica Horrocks
Typeset by J&M Typesetters

Printed and bound in Australia by Griffin Press, an Accredited ISO AS/NZS 14001:2004 Environmental Management System printer

ISBN: 9781925603378 (paperback)
ISBN: 9781925626414 (ebook)

A catalogue record for this book is available from the National Library of Australia

For Rachel, for Daniel, forever...

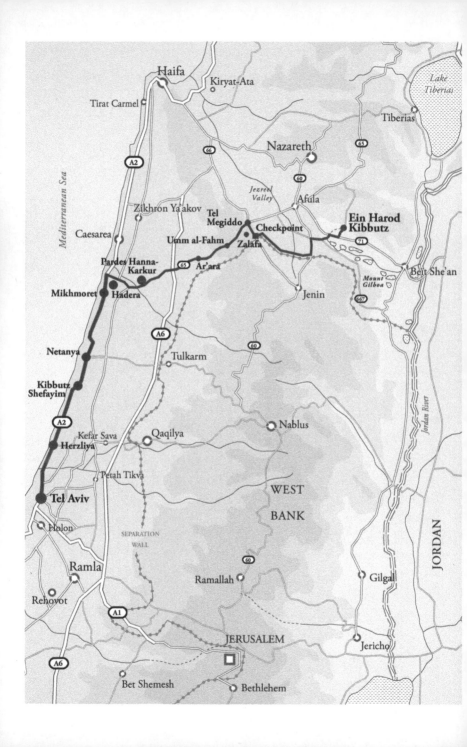

Saba is the Hebrew word
for grandfather

No, no, Mum. You don't have to wear a seatbelt. Not in wartime. You can push the seat back with that lever. Yes, like that. Just sit back, okay?

Can you hear Rufus yapping? I can see him in the rear-view mirror. He doesn't seem very happy that you're leaving.

How old is he again? Twelve? Thirteen?

Fifteen.

```
SCHOOL
REDUCE SPEED
```

Ouch! Sorry!

Are they new, those speed humps?

Yes, they're for—

Whoops, sorry, another one! I'd better watch out. This old wreck doesn't belong to me. It's my mate Yoni's rattletrap. You know who I mean? Yes, you do. Tall thin guy with red hair, crew cut. He's at uni with me. He left me the keys to his wheels when he was recruited. And to his apartment—so I'd drop by and water the plants. A two-bedroom. That's where we hid out in the beginning. At Yoni's.

Hey, so the kibbutz hasn't changed. Except for the speed humps...

> **OTHER ROUTES**
> Through traffic in 50 m

What a pity Dad didn't want to come with us. I tried to convince him while you were getting into the car. But he'd already put on his overalls and boots.

You don't just get up and go like that, and leave a farm...

Why are you always trying to let him off the hook?

I'm going to take the old Jenin road and go along the separation wall until Salem. If the traffic's okay we'll be in Tel Aviv in two hours.

Look, a poppy!

```
┌─────────────────────────────────┐
│              מעיין חרוד          │
│   3 km      عين جالوت            │
│           Ma'ayan Harod          │
└─────────────────────────────────┘
```

Don't be sad, Mum.

I'm not at all sad.

Well, I wonder what you would have done, if it had been up to you?

מעיין חרוד
عين جالوت
Ma'ayan Harod

Yaël and I had our backpacks ready. We'd turned off the water and electricity, per the decree. All we had to do was go and get Saba. I'd told him that we'd come by and pick him up around one o'clock. Yaël came with me. You know how well Saba got on with her. He used to call her 'my sweetheart'.

When we arrived at his place, at one o'clock,

we found him settled into his armchair, reading *Molloy*. In English. He jumped up to get us a drink. Lukewarm vodka. All the while talking about Samuel Beckett and James Joyce.

So we let him keep wandering off in his musings on *Ulysses* and the stream of consciousness and Beckett and 'the ambivalent relationship of his characters to reality'. We didn't dare interrupt. We understood, you know?

There'd been no air-raid sirens that day. No missile attacks. So he'd forgotten there was a war on.

We didn't have the courage, right then, to remind him.

Not because we were frightened of being pushy. Not at all! But because it did us good to listen to him, to hear him declare that writers talk too much about death. To enjoy his tasteless vodka. It did us good, too, to forget the war.

Have you never done that, pretended you're not part of what's happening around you? As if you were a character out of Beckett. To experience that feeling of insignificance. About everything.

As if you were Molloy.

Do you want me to turn on the aircon?

No?

Saba had turned off the TV, you know. He'd
turned it around to face the wall. As if it were
broken. Or had been put in the naughty corner. Yaël
noticed it first. I suggested we see what was wrong,
check the socket. As a joke. Yaël told me I was an
idiot. And Saba kept on with his spiel as if he hadn't
heard me. But the spell was broken. The spell cast
by *Ulysses*, by *Molloy*. So Yaël took Saba's hand and
asked him to stop talking.

And, guess what, he shut up.

All the same, it wasn't easy, getting down to the
business at hand.

7

To start with, Saba made me specify exactly which war we could possibly be talking about. As if he had lost count. And clarify who had made the first move. Fired the first shot.

He seemed to be highly amused by it.

When Yaël told him that this time things weren't looking good, he appeared not to understand what she was saying. She had to repeat it. Three times. Go into detail. Insist. She was on the verge of tears. And that's what finally made Saba assure her that he knew perfectly well which war she was talking about. And that we were going to win it, for sure.

While he was holding forth on the military tactics that needed to be employed, I took the opportunity to go and look for his travel bag in the bedroom.

Well, he had unpacked it all. Everything!

Dammit, I'd just been there the day before to help him get ready. He'd seemed thrilled when I told him we'd be going to your place, on the kibbutz, until things quietened down.

Who knows what had gone through his mind in the meantime. No way was he going to tell me. He was certain I'd figure it out for myself. Completely convinced.

You know, that sort of confidence makes you want to join the cause.

Yes, that's exactly it. It made me join the cause.

```
הר הגלבוע
جبال فقوعة
Mount Gilboa
(SCENIC ROUTE)
```

We could go via the hills...

You said we'd take the shortest route. Right above Jenin.

I would've liked to see the irises. They're in bloom now, aren't they?

Every year the same.

Never mind. We'll go the short way.

Like I said.

```
┌─────────────────────────┐
│                         │
│     The Spice Farm      │
│      RESTAURANT         │
│        150 m            │
│                         │
└─────────────────────────┘
```

This brings back memories, doesn't it?

Apparently they're going to reopen soon. Well, if the peace talks are successful…

Three days without air raids, the ceasefire seems to be holding.

Insha'Allah.

```
┌─────────────────────────┐
│      CLIENT PARKING     │
└─────────────────────────┘
```

So, I quickly packed up Saba's things again while Yaël explained to him that we had to stick to the time slot we'd been allocated, otherwise we'd be sent to a camp. A 'reception camp', she was careful to stipulate in her gentle voice.

Saba didn't protest. He picked up his copy of *Molloy* and put it under his arm, so he'd have something to read on the trip. Yaël washed the vodka glasses. And I locked up, per the decree. I'd already told Dad we were coming, remember? So he'd collect us from the bus station at Afula.

Yaël had made sandwiches for the trip.

We left, shunting Saba in front of us. We had to get a move on, as you can imagine.

Down in the street it was mayhem.

The army had distributed leaflets explaining how the evacuation of Tel Aviv would take place neighbourhood by neighbourhood, to avoid congestion. The military probably thought the traffic would evaporate simply because they had given the order. What a joke! The traffic jams, the honking horns, the swearing—it was all in full swing, even worse than usual. A bit like when everyone goes on holiday: suitcases lined up along the pavements, sleeping bags lashed to luggage racks, iceboxes, camping stoves, kids running around everywhere.

It was sort of cheerful.

Not too sad, anyway.

At every crossroad, soldiers were waving multi-coloured flags to direct the traffic. And the civil defence had set up spots to distribute bottles of mineral water. The ones with bite valve lids for marathon runners.

Saba was thrilled to be mixing with the crowd, roaming through the city when it was all abuzz. As you know, it's hard to freak out when you're walking the streets of Tel Aviv. Even when there's turmoil. You get anxious, of course. But less than in the suburbs or out in the countryside. A lot less. Not as anxious as when you're in Jerusalem, in any case.

Well, there's Dad! He's always worried sick.

He's a farmer.

And you, too—you worry. Because you live with him.

Even when the harvest is good.

Keep your eyes on the road, will you?

This is where we take a right.
    Watch out!
    Sorry, I turned too sharply.
    You can say that again!
    I was afraid I'd miss the turn-off.

We managed to catch our bus in the end.

It was jam-packed.

We rushed to the back row and stuck our bags under the seat in front. I suggested that Saba take the window. He didn't want to. He sat in the middle, facing the aisle. I was the one who sat by the window. Yaël ended up between us.

Once the last passengers were seated, a corporal arrived and stood next to the driver. She was quite big. Blonde. A bit shy. She blew into a microphone a couple of times, then launched into the safety demonstration. Yes, yes, the one everyone has seen a hundred times. And that no one ever remembers.

She recited the safety instructions from memory.

In a matter-of-fact tone. Like a robot. In the event of an air raid en route…And she slipped on the gas mask and hazmat suit. Like this, and like this…In slow motion. Making sure she didn't mess up her bun.

You'd have thought she was a flight attendant before take-off.

It was right then, just as the corporal was showing us how to close the velcro fastening from bottom to top, that Saba got off the bus. He said he'd only be a minute. That he'd be back straightaway. He left carrying his copy of *Molloy*.

Yaël leapt up. She reached Saba in no time. He wasn't running. I saw Yaël pat his cheek. Before I caught up with them.

> SPEED LIMIT 30 KM/H

Have you noticed how the light bounces off the Separation Wall at this time of day? When I drove by this morning, on my way over, the road was in shadow, the sun still low behind the hills. Now the cement is in full sunlight.

It's blinding?

Yes, a bit.

Saba told us that under no circumstances was he getting back on the bus. He had changed his mind. We could just leave without him. He asked me to give him back the keys to his apartment. I refused, of course. The police were combing all the evacuated buildings. And the car parks, courtyards, public gardens. Whether he slept in his place or outside, sooner or later he would be picked up by a patrol. And sent off to a relocation facility.

I didn't tell him about the encampments set up by the government in the Negev. He loves the desert, camping out under the stars. But I told him about the one in Nablus. Huge, overcrowded. The one closest to Tel Aviv. Also the safest. At least as long as the enemy held off bombing the Palestinian Authority. Saba thought it was a bit rich that the Palestinians would be our human shield.

I could tell he was taken aback by what I was saying, and starting to have second thoughts.

The overcrowding, the communal showers, the barbed-wire fences, it all brought back bad memories. Of course. The word 'refugee' has always infuriated him, so I said it to him over and over, to get on his nerves.

Refugee, refugee, refugee...

And then I made the point about how lucky he was to be able to get away from this every-man-for-himself chaos and go to his daughter's. On the kibbutz. Out of harm's way. I used the expression 'safe haven'. Which he was not happy about. I told him it would be a chance for you two finally to make your peace with each other.

I might as well have been talking to a brick wall.

Like that one.

Yes, I suppose so.

In the meantime, the female soldier was shouting from the top of the bus steps. She couldn't come down because she was tangled up in the polypropylene wrapping of the hazmat suit. The bus engine started to throb.

The upshot was that I lost my temper.

I called Saba a selfish old man. I accused him of putting our lives at risk. Which was a big mistake, because Saba immediately worked out that, if he didn't budge, Yaël and I would end up staying with him.

In any case, I couldn't just ditch him.

Yes, you should have, Naor. For Yaël's sake.

Yaël? I wouldn't be surprised if she was in cahoots with him, right from the start.

I mean it!

When the bus started moving, they both had the same crestfallen smile. Coyly contrite, if you know what I mean.

And what about you?

I ran after our bus, of course! As fast as I could. It was leaving with our bags.

Yeah, right, you can laugh.

Our identity papers, our laptops, the flash drives. My PlayStation console. Everything, really. Saba's medication.

And the sandwiches.

It's not funny, Mum.

I ran like crazy. I only gave up when the bus turned onto the ring road. I was out of breath. A bloke came over and asked if I was all right, if I needed help. He looked like a cop. And I looked pretty dodgy. I don't remember what I said to get rid of him. And then I went back down the boulevard. It took me a while to make my way through, against the flow, everyone heading the other way.

Saba and Yaël were waiting for me on a bench. They didn't look too worried that I'd come back empty-handed. Straightaway I got my mobile out of my pocket and sent a text to Dad to let him know that the bus had left without us, and asking him to collect our bags when it arrived. Then I sent a selfie of the three of us sitting on the bench—with a smiley emoji. So that you wouldn't worry too much. Because of the time difference with Los Angeles, Yaël didn't contact her parents until later that evening. And she didn't want to talk to them over the phone, or hear them making a fuss.

We stayed sitting there for a while, watching the cars and trucks filing past. The city emptying. We were like three little old people getting some fresh air, not speaking, not moving.

A bit further down the road, a news crew was filming the scene with a wide-angle lens. As you can imagine, there were journalists everywhere. One of the reporters, the one holding the microphone, came and asked us—in English, politely—to move away. We were in their field of vision.

As we were standing up, he noticed the book Saba had in his hand. The copy of *Molloy*. He was so impressed that he asked Saba to say a few words about Operation Noah's Ark. To which Saba retorted that he was not at all happy about the term, that it was inappropriate, as usual, and that the analogy between biological warheads and the Great Flood was completely ludicrous. *Utterly kitsch, really*, was what he said. Far too Cecil B. DeMille and Ridley Scott for his liking. All in all, he added, things would have proceeded better if the covenant had been made with Lot rather than Noah. Given that Tel Aviv was Sodom and Gomorrah. So, more like Fellini. Or even Emir Kusturica. He actually said that. In perfect English. His references to the seventh art were his way of introducing me, his grandson, brilliant student in the cinema department at Tel Aviv University, assistant film editor of several short films, one of which had won a prize at last year's Docaviv film festival. At which point the journalist quickly thanked Saba and returned to his position behind his camera.

Behind him the last cars were heading up the boulevard.

The little we overheard of what he was saying didn't sound too bad. His voice took on a slightly annoyed, almost croaky tone, when he said the words 'the Israelis', or 'the Jewish state'. It seemed to bother him.

Yaël wandered off while he was talking. She walked along the pavements, then reappeared in camera range. She held her arms in the air, the sky her witness, grimacing and gesticulating like a silent actress. You should have seen how beautiful she was. A tragedienne. With her pale skin, her curly pitch-black hair, her swaying body. Her head thrown back, very Eastern European. Very Sarah Bernhardt.

I grabbed my mobile to immortalise the moment on video. And post it online.

When Yaël came back, Saba kissed her hand. I didn't dare to.

It was she who came and kissed me on the cheek. Like a naughty little girl who wants to be forgiven.

The special correspondents looked puzzled.

I wonder if they edited out her performance afterwards. Or if they kept it as some integral element of the news report.

Did you know that the 'B' in Cecil B. DeMille stands for Blount? Cecil Blount! Can you believe it?

Maybe I should turn on the radio. We haven't passed anyone for a while. Apart from that shepherd and his goats. What if there's an air raid happening right now?

So what if there's an air raid?

You're right. There's nowhere to hide around here.

Yaël had kept the keys with her, in the pocket of her trench coat. Saba's keys, the keys to Yoni's place, all clipped onto my keyring. Three furnished apartments available in the heart of Tel Aviv. Unheard of!

Hoping we'd get arrested, I thought at first that we should head back to Saba's. After all, that's what Saba wanted. To go home.

Yaël suggested we go to Yoni's. There'd be tinned food there, she said. Perhaps even some frozen food. Granted, I did empty the freezer at our place before we left. And you know Saba, he eats out most of the time. At the Yemeni place below his apartment.

We were starting to get a bit peckish.

Saba immediately agreed with Yaël. He smelled a rat, you see. They would be going through his street with a fine-tooth comb that very evening. Whereas Yoni's side of town, the Florentin neighbourhood, had already been cleared out—the evacuation oper-ations had begun in the areas of Tel Aviv where people were less civic-minded.

It was getting dark. The film crew had packed up.

There was almost no one left on the boulevard.

Yaël and Saba hadn't moved. They were waiting for me to give the order to get going. So I said

Onwards! Or maybe *Off we go!* I can't remember.

I decided we should avoid going anywhere near the sea, the main thoroughfares, or the lighted areas. That was my gut instinct. I no longer wanted us to get caught. Right from the start, of course, we'd been engaged in illegal behaviour. Dissidence.

Saba played the fugitive brilliantly. Better than Yaël and me. It was obvious straightaway: he started walking stealthily, light-footed all of a sudden. He was reliving his youth, his years in the underground. Before he was captured and...

CHECKPOINT IN 1500M

We went along the back alleys in the lower part of the city. And then through the Carmel Market, where the smell of spices still lingered.

The 'civil population' had well and truly disappeared. And not only them. There wasn't a single cat hanging around among the abandoned crates. Not even a rat. 'They're hiding in the sewers,' Saba said, a worried look on his face. And for good reason. The minute we left the souk and came out in the residential district of Neve Tzedek, the sirens started blaring.

We rushed to the first doorway we could find. You needed an access code to get through the entrance to the building. We crouched there on the spot. I wasn't sure crouching was exactly what we should be doing. It was probably better to stay upright, against the wall. Yaël held my hand, but not tightly. And then the sky lit up.

There were explosions everywhere, Mum.

From where we were standing, we couldn't see much, which made us feel safer. Like when kids shut their eyes. And then a rocket ripped through the corner of sky that we could glimpse, piercing the night with a white vapour trail. Very low. It had passed through the defence shield, its boosters shrieking so loudly we thought it was heading straight for us. But it kept going and struck a bit further on, two or three hundred metres away, with an almighty *boom*. We lurched as it smashed into the building. The InterContinental Hotel. Shards of glass landed at our feet.

When the hotel caved in, I felt nauseous. Yes,

acid in my gut at the sight of it collapsing, slowly, like a sinking ship. We didn't hear any screaming. No cries for help. The hotel was probably empty. Or else everyone was dead.

More detonations reverberated. Further south. And then there was silence again. And Yaël let go of my hand.

Saba craned forward. All he managed to say, his nose in the air, was that there was a smell of burning but it wasn't chemical. I was inclined to inform him that you can't smell germ warfare. But, actually, I wasn't sure.

There was also a salty fragrance carried by a gentle breeze coming from the sea.

CHECKPOINT IN 1000 M

I wanted to take a photo of the debris. To put it on YouTube. Yaël stopped me. It was prohibited. It would amount to revealing the coordinates of the strike. I quickly put away my phone.

I had almost committed an act of high treason.

We only left our shelter when we noticed a cat

on the pavement opposite. It had emerged precisely at the end of the mandatory ten minutes you have to wait after an explosion. We set off again towards the Florentin neighbourhood, heading for Yoni's.

At every street corner, I expected to see people. But, apart from the flashing lights of the fire trucks and the police cars blinking in the distance, there was no sign of life.

We couldn't have been the only ones who had stayed in the city on the sly. So where were the others?

We kept moving as if in a dream.

Some billboards were still lit up. There was the one of the latest Mazda charging across Arizona. And the El Al promotion for a direct flight, Tel Aviv–Colombo. Valid till the end of the month. And an ad for Phoenix, 'the best life insurance'.

The traffic lights were still working.

On the corner of Abarbanel and Salame streets, Saba took my arm. Impatiently or affectionately, I'm not sure. I could feel the fear emanating from his body. He was almost dancing.

Did you foresee that he might refuse to evacuate?

Hadn't you?

CHECKPOINT IN 500 M

And that we would end up being his accomplices?

The police called us in the next morning, your father and me. To hand over statements from the bus driver and the corporal. An inspector asked us if we knew where you had gone, if we had any news. It was awkward.

I was worried that Saba wouldn't cope with getting arrested. Caught. Taken to the police station. I thought it might bring back his fears from the past. That's why I didn't disclose where we were hiding out. Not even to you.

Are you angry with me for that?

No, Naor, I'm not angry with you at all.

You look like it.

I'm jealous, that's all.

CHECKPOINT

Here's the checkpoint.

When I came through this morning, I didn't have any hard-copy ID at all. No statutory declaration of loss, no temporary papers. Just the QR ID code to scan from my phone. There were two soldiers on duty. Half-asleep. I smiled at them. That was enough.

I wonder how they decide who to carry out checks on. Who to body-search, who not to. Do you think it's about what you look like?

You know exactly what I think about that.

STOP

Did you bring some ID?

I thought a smile would be enough.

Shalom, corporal. We're from Ein Harod Kibbutz. And my mother never smiles.

```
                    חל מגידו
        4 km        مجيدو
                    Tel Megiddo
```

It's beautiful, this winter sun.

The olive trees. The cypresses. The hills.

You know, Cecil B. DeMille filmed *The Ten Commandments* on location in Egypt. He wanted everything to be authentic. Beginning with the light. If he didn't part the waters of the Red Sea for the second time, it was simply due to a budget shortage. He had to resign himself to filming tons of water gushing from huge tanks erected on the set in the backlot at Paramount. I'm talking about the 1956 version. In VistaVision. With

Charlton Heston in the role of Moses.

He made another, silent version in 1923, for which he had temples and statues erected on the shores of the Pacific Ocean, near Seal Beach, in California. A few years ago, bulldozers unearthed a large sphinx made out of chipboard. Buried in the dunes. Cecil Blount was on our first-semester syllabus. Just before the war started and the teacher had to go back to his unit. For his last class he screened the 1934 *Cleopatra*, with Claudette Colbert.

I had hardly ever seen anything of such sheer purity.

Saba was born the same year. In 1934.

Really!

Didn't you know?

Not exactly. I mean, I hadn't put two and two together. He has always made an effort not to look his age.

Like all old people.

Do you think he's playing at being a rebel so people think he's younger?

Just like you're playing the rebel so you come across as more mature...

Well, what do you know, it's worked for both of us. Right from the word go.

I noticed how Saba became more animated as we made our way through the city. And I felt myself becoming more mature with each step. Yaël too, in a way. After that night, she no longer spoke like a young girl. It was as if she had suddenly grown up.

She began talking to us like a mother hen, which infuriated me. She sounded just like Grandma. Without the accent, obviously, or the slight tremor of the lips.

Grandma? Do you remember her voice?

And the way she was always wiping my cheeks, my mouth, my chin. And wiping my nose even when it wasn't running.

Apparently you two got on well.

Why do you say that?

Saba told me that you always took her side whenever he and Grandma had an argument.

What on earth was he on about, the old liar?

What do you mean? It's not true?

They never argued. Grandma gave in to him on everything.

There are so many lies inside a family, aren't there?

Secrets.

מעלה עירון

معاليه عيرون

Ma'ale Iron–Djabal 'Ara

Two names for the same place.

As soon as we got to Yoni's, we closed the blinds and descended on the kitchen.

In the sideboard, there were tins of tuna and sardines. Packets of quinoa. A bag of lentils. Enough for us to hold out for three days, no longer.

We stayed indoors for those three days, waiting until the evacuation was over. And for the patrols to ease off. We didn't sleep a wink the first night; we were too excited. We talked about the rocket that struck the InterContinental Hotel, about the blast from the explosion that hit us square in the face. We each took turns talking about it, recounting what we had experienced down there in the doorway, what we had seen, while the other two waited patiently to fill in the gaps. That's how the memory of what happened took shape, how it registered itself in our minds. Shot by shot, like editing a film. But the more we reconstructed it, piece by piece, the less real it seemed. It ended up too clear-cut, if you see what I mean. Reality is more fuzzy.

We each drew our own conclusions, expressed our own opinion for the benefit of the esteemed assembly. Calmly, and in a dignified manner. Just like at the United Nations.

I spoke first, and said that the good thing about rockets and bombs, in spite of everything, was that they brought people together. In the heat of the moment, at least. And it shook up the routine. To which Saba retorted that there was nothing more banal than a state of emergency. Nothing more commonplace than disaster and bloodshed. He talked about the millions of animals that devour each other every day, every hour. And he talked about fish farming, which he called routine slaughter. And he accused God of having made a mess of things. All the while admitting that it was ever so slightly exhilarating having a constant threat hanging over our lives. Over life.

Yaël branded our talk 'moronic and vapid'. And 'downright perverse'. She chastised us for encouraging each other to 'systematically play the fool'. Saba was not impressed by the accusation. He could be accused of anything you like, but not 'systematic'. 'I beg to differ,' he began to say. In English. To emphasise that he was offended. The discussion was going to end up turning nasty.

Fortunately, the air-raid sirens started wailing. Just in the nick of time.

They wailed almost the whole night.

The enemy was hopping mad. Because of the evacuation. You could feel it in the way the bombs arrived from every direction. Sporadic. In fits and starts. Shots in the dark.

Yoni lives in one of those old buildings where there is no shelter as such. Not even a cellar. And definitely no storage spaces with reinforced walls. Every time the air-raid siren rang out, we went and huddled in the stairwell, sitting on the steps.

At times like that, I really wanted to smoke. But there was no tobacco. I haven't taken it up again since. Did you notice?

In the heat of the moment, you aren't really frightened. You trust in your reflexes. It's only once you're crouched down, lying low, that you start to think about it. You get a little lump in your throat. And you crave a cigarette.

On that first night, we followed the sequence of military operations online. Yaël and I checked Facebook and Twitter, brushing aside the jibes from Saba, who despises all that.

I had a quick look at online survival handbooks, at documentaries on germ warfare and even at clips from sci-fi films. When Saba saw what I was doing, he put in a request for Fritz Lang's *Metropolis*. He was sure I'd get it wrong. Or at least he hoped I would. A film over two and half hours long, made more than a hundred years ago! So when he saw the first shots of *Metropolis* scrolling across the screen of my phone, that shut him up for a bit. In spite of everything.

We went back to the apartment during lulls in the attacks. The windowpanes were vibrating: there was a deafening roar of throbbing car engines coming from the north. From the wealthy suburbs.

Thousands of four-wheel drives and hybrids leaving Bavli and Shikun Lamed that very night. And armoured vehicles taking their place, to provide security surveillance for the luxury apartment buildings and villas, to guard against looting. What a noble gesture to protect the country's heritage.

So there you go: we were right to set up in one of the ugliest spots in Tel Aviv, where there was nothing to keep an eye on or protect. There were no tanks outside our apartment. Not even a police van.

In the beginning, we still had to be careful. We didn't open the blinds, and we checked there was no one around before running water in the bathtub or flushing the toilet. It was Yaël's job to keep a lookout. She would open the door to the landing and stick her nose out. She can hear a pin drop.

From the second night on, we became so paranoid that we left our phones turned off most of the time—out of fear they would track us with their sensors, or whatever else they had. We only turned them on to let you and Yaël's parents know that we were okay.

Afterwards, there was no point with all that

carry-on. All the networks crashed, one by one. First the wifi, then the landline. And there were no more patrols.

It was official: the city was empty.

The missile attacks became less sustained, although more concentrated. Targeting the Defence Ministry, which they had not a hope in hell of reaching—thirty-six feet underground. It's true there wasn't much else to zero in on once the civilian population had left.

The target had vanished, right under the nose of the enemy—thanks to a simple and enormously silly trick: leaving the place.

Do you reckon the exits in the underground headquarters of the IDF are signposted with little luminous panels like in cinemas—with that stylised human shape running behind an arrow?

We'll fill up at the petrol station opposite the prison.
And get a coffee. What do you think?

I'm in.

This evacuation from Tel Aviv, which I thought
was so cool, well, Saba was against it all along.

He was deeply disgusted by the whole thing.

But that's not why he decided to resist, is it?

No, you're right. Even if he wasn't okay with it,
he would have obeyed and complied. Like the old
soldier that he is.

You're right. It was about a totally different thing.
How did you know?

43

A white coffee, please. Nice and milky.

I'll have an espresso.

It's been ages since I've said that. An espresso.

When we left our hideout for the first time, that's what we found the most upsetting: the empty café terraces, the table legs chained, padlocked. The chairs stacked up. It was heartbreaking. You can't imagine it. You'd have to be a city person to understand. I mean, for it to affect you so much.

Everything was shut. Like on Holocaust Memorial Day, or Yom Kippur.

I thought about those who had left, about those who were somewhere else. I thought about you.

About Yoni and about all the soldiers.

I would have liked to go to the front, too. To have been called up. Instead of having 'health issues', as Yaël said.

And how are you going with all that?

Not bad. Not bad at all. If you take into account that I've gone the last few months without any treatment. Not even anti-inflammatories. I haven't had a pain in my gut once.

Sugar?

No, thank you.

Saba has kept well, too. Without his medications. Yaël's the one who came down with a cold. Miss I-never-get-sick! She started coughing as soon as we ventured outside. But the breeze was playing havoc with the slagheaps left after the explosions. We were swallowing ashes. It was foul. In fact, that constant stink of stubbed-out cigarettes helped me to stop smoking.

Dad will be happy. I forgot to tell him the good news.

What good news?

That I don't smoke anymore!

Have you finished your coffee? Was it okay?
    Do you want anything else?
    No, thank you.

It's great to be able to fill up at the normal price. The cans of petrol in the boot cost me an arm and a leg. On the black market.

Are you in your seat properly?

You don't have to wear a seatbelt, Mum. I've already told you.

I bought some crisps while you were in the bathroom. And a bottle of water. A big one.

The power cuts and water stoppages became more frequent and lasted longer. You can do without petrol and electricity. And without the internet. But water is a whole other story. There was less and less of it. Fortunately, we didn't have to go far to find some.

There is a grocery shop around the corner from Yoni's place. A sort of minimart. It has a metal security shutter at the front. But not out the back, where it opens onto a little courtyard. All we had to do was kick the door down.

We did our shopping and took everything up to the apartment, in three trips. The first for the bottles of mineral water. The second for the biscuits, tinned food and vodka. The last for toiletries and cleaning products.

The neighbourhood was deserted. No cops. No soldiers on patrol.

The alarm didn't go off, because there was no power. And the video surveillance wasn't working either. But we kept a low profile anyway.

Because of the drones.

When we came back the next day, to get garbage bags and candles, there was almost nothing left on the shelves. Someone had come through after us.

From then on, we would often arrive at a shop where others had already stocked up and we would have to make do with the leftovers.

We hardly ever ran into the 'others'. They were

being careful too. The only time we encountered someone, we just kept going, without saying a word, without even glancing at each other.

See, those of us who had stayed were connected, but not reliant on one another.

We knew that each squat owed its survival to its size. The fewer people it had, the more difficult it was to locate. And the less likely it was that its members would end up quarrelling. We three, for example, became closer together each day.

We used eau de toilette for two weeks, before daring to head for the sea to wash ourselves.

And we went to the toilet downstairs, in the courtyard, above a drain. For a whole lot of reasons, this was more dangerous than you might imagine.

One evening when I was crouching there, in the middle of a shit, a jackal came and stood right in front of me. Its yellow eyes shone in the twilight. We stayed there like that for a while, facing each other. Without moving. Without making the slightest sound. And then the jackal moved off, continuing on its way as if nothing had happened. Just like the other squatter we'd passed. Between the two of us, the jackal and me, there had been the same silent understanding. An implicit sense of fellowship.

That was the first jackal. Afterwards there were others. Many others. They'd spread the word. We ended up having to get rid of our rubbish further and further away. They dug it up each time, which meant we were in danger of being exposed. On the other hand, they got rid of the rats, which swarmed out at night in packs to make raids, emboldened by the empty streets.

The jackals also devoured the ducks and geese in the park by the Yarkon River. They hunted down the feral cats and stray dogs. They turned the whole ecosystem upside down. Or perhaps they restored it. Who knows.

In any case, the city divided itself into new territories—for animals only, not for humans.

The creatures that best established their dominion in the end were the crows. Because the jackals got sick from eating city rats rather than field rats. Or simply from stuffing themselves.

Which was never going to happen to you...

On the contrary. I was hungrier than ever. Guess

what, war takes the edge off Crohn's disease. It provides a kind of remission.

Your sister rang me last night. The news has hit her pretty hard.

I know. She told me.

She's going to try to join us, if she can...

Yes, if she can.

Driving is still risky. Especially with little children.

The main thing is that they're okay. I was really worried about them.

It was hard not knowing anything.

The networks had gone down. But shortwave worked. Radio, of course. It allowed us to keep track of the troop movements, of how the war was developing, of the numbers of dead and the wounded. The news invariably ended with the weather forecasts. Just like normal. A decision no doubt taken by the production people. Afterwards, it became harder and harder to pick up the signal. Because of the magnetic screens that the army had set up around the zone. So, bit by bit, we were cut off from the rest of the world.

We're nearly at Umm al-Fahm.

Umm, I know that. It means mother. And *fahm*, what does that mean?

Fahm, *that's* pecham *in Hebrew. Charcoal.*

Mother of Charcoal?

Yes, that's it.

אֻם אל-פַחְם

أمّ الفحم

Umm al-Fahm

What we missed most in the beginning was a change of clothes. It would have been completely reckless to head across town to our place to get clothes. It just wasn't worth it. So, we decided to make do with what we had to hand. The stuff we found in the wardrobes didn't fit any of us. And it was all hideous. Especially the T-shirts. We all dressed as Yoni for three or four days, until we ran out of clothes, and went and broke into a clothes shop. And then another one. We had to keep changing our outfits because there wasn't enough running water to do any washing.

In the first shop, Yaël chose understated colours from Thierry Mugler's autumn collection, and a

silk Issey Miyake scarf. She made me try on poly-
ester pants and patterned shirts. As if I were her
dress-up doll. And Saba found a baggy beige suit.
Very Hemingway.

All dressed up, we didn't feel like going back
to the apartment straightaway. We went for a walk
along Rothschild Boulevard. There was a light
shower that didn't last long, a few tentative drops,
typical for the end of October. I walked arm in arm
with Yaël. Saba walked ahead of us at a jaunty pace.
The coat-tails of his jacket flapped in the wind like
wings.

We were walking. He was flying.

For Yaël and me, staying in deserted Tel Aviv was
an act of resistance, of hanging on, standing firm.
Whereas for Saba, it was about letting go, giving up.
The doctors had advised him that he wouldn't make
it through the winter.

The doctors tell him that every year.

Yes, but this time he decided to believe them.
He told me. Because he could feel death silently
creeping up on him. And he had to prepare.

The truth is that I was the one with blind faith.

Tel Aviv would never give in, never!

Yaël laughed at my patriotism. She labelled it 'municipal Zionism'. It's true that there is something chauvinistic about Tel Avivians. Separatist, even. We can give back a lot of things: the Golan Heights, the Samarian Hills, the Sea of Galilee. Negotiate the lot. Even the Wailing Wall. After all, we did without them for centuries. And plenty of Jews, from London to Manhattan, still do without them. But under no circumstances are we giving up one inch of old Tel Aviv. Not Masaryk Square. Not Montefiore Street. And especially not Banana Beach!

Not that bit of beach from where you can feast your eyes on the skyline of Jaffa while sipping on a beer. And where Arab women go swimming, fully dressed, in among the surfers and girls in G-strings.

Tell me why I should evacuate Tel Aviv.

To save Jerusalem? Another city.

But not a city like any other.

Some safe haven! One hell of a refuge for the Hebrew people!

Jerusalem is too demanding. Too holy. It takes over your soul. I've never really felt at ease there.

Tel Aviv is much more accommodating. Reassuring. It's a sanctuary where Israelis themselves find refuge, whether they're Jewish or not. Where the restaurants are open late. Where you refuse to define yourself according to a conflict.

Others do that for you.

When they think about you, when they look at you, they only see this damned 'conflict'. They identify you with it. Or at least with the idea they have of it. And they talk to you about peace. That's all they talk about. The conflict, negotiations, peace. And, idiot that you are, instead of signing peace agreements, you stay lolling in your deckchair, sipping beer, checking out the girls in G-strings or chadors.

You waste your time living.

That's what the three of us did that day: wasted our time.

Yaël and I followed Saba along the rows of trees down Rothschild Boulevard. Saba acting the dandy, so proud of his new suit, its wide beige coat-tails fluttering in the breeze. Saba, whose refusal to evacuate had nothing to do with the fighting. Or any sort of conflict.

Later on, we returned several times to that boulevard with its old-fashioned, colonial charm. An ill-defined coupling of Havana with pre-war Berlin. Not a huge success. Totally fanciful. Perfect for a film set.

I couldn't resist.

What do you mean?

We shot the opening scene of our film there.

We called it *Evacuation.*

עַרְעָרה
عرعرة
Ar'ara

One more Arab village to go through. Then we'll get onto the highway.

Is it a documentary?

Not at all. Every sequence has been edited. Orchestrated down to the last detail. Every word of the script has been meticulously drafted. We had to do a few rewrites. Yaël and Saba had to rehearse before the shoot. I wanted them to be perfect, as characters. And I had to be, too. In my own role as grandson, and as director.

Can I see the film?

It's all there, on my phone. I haven't deleted anything. Or edited out anything.

I wasn't brave enough to do that.

> כפר קרע
> كفر قرع
> Kafr Qara

Look at that Bedouin guy over there. What's he selling? Pita bread with thyme?

Do you want some?

No, thanks, I'm not hungry.

Me neither. I could have got hold of a state-of-the-art camera, gone and nicked one from the Sony shop. But sophisticated equipment wasn't right. Not for the frame of mind we'd been thrust into with the evacuation. Nor for what Saba was going through, which he wanted us to experience too. He wanted to teach us, by revealing himself, by setting an example. Starting with losing the habit of all forms of comfort.

And I don't just mean doing our washing by hand and using candles for lighting. I mean our ideas. About life. About Israel. I mean the war, too.

But also the feeling we had there, in Florentin, of being safer than anywhere else. What I mean is our sense of uncertainty, our doubts. About what we're doing here, us, Jews. But also the inevitability of it. I mean the isolation. And also the universal nature of it. Our lonely universality. Our universal loneliness. I mean all these incoherent things. Our refusal to succumb to logic. To history. I mean an old man. His fanatical obstinacy not to be evacuated from Tel Aviv, coupled with his completely calm acceptance of death, which Saba did not bother to explain to us, to formulate in so many words. Because using words would have been too convenient. Just like a state-of-the-art camera would have been for the film we were in the process of shooting.

> IRON INTERCHANGE
> (to Highway 6)

Actually, I think it's better if we take Highway 65 until Caesarea, and then go along by the coast. Highway 6 could be congested. I got caught there on the way through. By a military convoy. Tank transporters that took up two lanes and didn't exceed thirty kilometres an hour.

And, anyway, the landscape is more attractive on the 65.

You're quiet.

I'm thinking about Yaël.

Without her, you know…

I know.

It's not like we couldn't have coped without her. Trust me, Saba and I would have muddled through fine. The thing was, we wanted to impress her. Saba, especially, wanted to amaze her.

He's always been a show-off.

You're telling me! He tried to have one over me even when I was a little boy. To impress me. But with Yaël it was different.

He used to give her gifts.

At first, he wasn't sure what she'd like. I never really knew myself. I mucked up so many times. Even with flowers: 'Torn out of the ground to die a horrible death in a vase.' So it was softly-softly for him.

He took her to his favourite places in Tel Aviv. Parks at the end of dead-end streets. Art galleries set up among warehouses and garages in the lower town. Converted cafés in disused clothing factories and carpentry workshops. Places with a past. Run-down, squalid businesses. Haberdasheries and hardware shops from another age that were still in operation. Neighbourhood synagogues: Turkish, Polish, Yemeni, Bulgarian, Uzbek, Iraqi. As they walked, he read her passages from *Molloy*, recited poems by David Avidan, hummed tunes that popped into his head, songs he hadn't sung for years. And, when I showed up with my idea for a film, he fell for it—hook, line and sinker.

He started to put on airs, to make a spectacle of himself. Right from the first sequences. Like the one where he smashes the glass doors of the Helena Rubinstein Pavilion for Contemporary Art and drags Yaël inside among the damaged installations. The stacks of Warhol and Basquiat lithographs, destroyed by mould. The twisted, crushed submachine guns by Igael Tumarkin, all rusted now. The huge canvases by Menashe Kadishman, coming out of their frames, covered in dust. Stored there for the duration of the war.

Yaël played along straightaway, pouting and grimacing in front of the pictures. Whirling like a crazy person around the sculptures. In the meantime, I was trying to work out the right angle, the depth of field, the correct lighting, while bitterly regretting the whole idea of the film. From then on, you see, everything seemed phoney, too affected—our gestures, our expressions, our silences. Even when we weren't filming. But it was too late to turn back.

FLORENTIN—ROOF-TERRACE OF
YONI'S BUILDING—DUSK

Trestle-table set up among the solar hot-water panels
and the satellite dishes.

White tablecloth, candelabra.

No flowers.

Saba enters, wearing a baggy beige suit.
Performing the gestures of a maître d', he sets
the table with plates and serviettes, and lights the
candelabra.

Yaël enters, holding a basket of dried fruit.

Saba takes the basket, places it on the table, turns
around, bows, kisses Yaël's hand. Then he uncorks
the champagne.

POP!

Air-raid sirens go off. The sky lights up. As Saba
proposes a toast.

Can you believe that Saba was determined to celebrate Yaël's birthday on top of the building—beneath the canopy of heaven and the bombs, as he said. And that Yaël thought it was a great idea.

She helped Saba carry up the table and the crockery and cutlery. A bucket to pretend that we had ice. And the nine-branched candelabra that Yoni uses during Hanukkah.

When everything was ready, Yaël went over and leaned against the roof railing. Saba practised saying his lines about ten times.

But, there you go, that night there was no air-raid.

Yaël and Saba asked me to film anyway. They were cross when I said no. I had to explain to them that, in the absence of any bombing, there was not enough light. That it was all about the light levels.

We still opened the champagne. Yaël blew out the candles that I had put on a marzipan cake. And Saba proposed his toast.

We stayed on the roof until late, before going back downstairs.

We stared at the stars for a long time, at the unclouded night, hoping for a blazing trail to streak across the sky so that we could film a few shots.

Wasn't Yaël frightened of the missiles?

Yes, of course she was.

But less afraid than she was of a predicted death, like Saba's.

Or the slow agony of a flower in a vase.

```
                              פרדס חנה
              3 km          دیس حنه کرکور
                           Pardes Hanna
```

Are you crying, Naor?

It'll pass.

פרדס חנה-כרכור
ديس حنه كركور
Pardes Hanna-Karkur

There were no air raids the next two nights either. None of the loud explosions we'd been hearing in the distance, from the direction of Ben Gurion Airport. Not even a helicopter overhead. So we decided to go home, return to our own apartments.

We cleaned Yoni's place, tidied up and left him a thankyou note.

We crossed the city without a problem. But the closer we got to our neighbourhood, the more damage there was. Obviously. So close to the IDF headquarters.

Just opposite, the old buildings of Sarona hadn't withstood the blasts. And one of the Gindi shopping-mall towers was lying full-length right in the middle of the landscaped gardens. It had landed directly on the pedestrian strip, as if deliberately avoiding the flowerbeds. A bit further on, the roof of the delicatessen market had a huge round crater in it, still smoking. Whereas ten metres or so along, on the other side of the boulevard, the Ministry of Defence was intact, its facade of safety glass sparkling in the sunshine.

I have never understood why the military staff head-quarters were right in the heart of Tel Aviv. It's absurd.

Surreal, you mean.

No, insane.

Perhaps it's because there is no real rearguard here. Only a frontline.

You sound just like your grandfather!

Rather than like you?

Or Yaël.

Please, Mum.

Forgive me.

There's no rearguard. There never has been.

Neither here, nor anywhere. No more than in Carthage or in Vietnam. War is for everyone, civilians as well as the military. Even animals—hey, what about the ones in Hiroshima Zoo!

Calm down, Naor.

Okay, okay, my turn to ask forgiveness.

Anyway, we felt as if we were turning up to a forward post, a position that needed holding, rather than returning home to the fold.

A feeling that was quickly reinforced when we arrived at our apartments. The windows had been blown out. Every window pane in the neighbourhood was shattered.

Two doves had made their nest in my living room. And shat everywhere.

At Saba's place, the first rains of the season had soaked the rugs, the armchairs, the books. There were only a few volumes in a reasonable enough condition to take with us. I suggested we break into a bookshop and pick up a few new releases. Saba said no, he would rather reread texts he'd already enjoyed, and study them in depth.

'Revise them,' he said.

I thought we'd take a few things with us, clothes, toiletries. But, since equipping ourselves from luxury boutiques, the three of us had become too choosy to use our old stuff.

All Yaël took with her were her paintbrushes, tubes of watercolour paint, pots of acrylic paint. And three or four clean canvases, not too big, easy to carry. I didn't take anything. The things I would like to have taken were too heavy, too cumbersome. And Saba didn't want to take his old typewriter, the Olivetti. On the other hand, he insisted on carrying Yaël's easel and palettes on his back, tied to his shoulders.

With his beige suit and his Panama hat, he looked like Renoir heading off to paint outdoors.

You knew he would like to have been a painter?

Instead of a writer.

At one point, he also dreamed of being a jazz musician.

We returned to Yoni's, feeling foolish. We'd thought about squatting in a more spacious dwelling, more practical. We had plenty to choose from. I don't know why we didn't in the end. We kept putting it off until later.

Walking back towards Florentin, we had the same sensation we'd had going the other way—of going home. Odd, don't you think?

The weather was so glorious we decided to take Rothschild Boulevard. It was deserted, silent and bathed in sunshine.

Saba was walking in front, as usual, striding along the wide central path bordered by trees and benches.

All of a sudden, he stopped, and signalled for us to stop too. He stood frozen to the spot, Yaël's easel still on his back, and pointed towards the patches of grass in the middle of the pathway.

A gazelle was grazing. Right there, halfway along the boulevard. A single gazelle.

It raised its head, hesitating, tensed for a second, on the alert. Then took flight.

It disappeared in a flash, so fast that we wondered if we'd really seen it.

Perhaps it was a mirage.

We're near the coast now.

Yaël started painting that very afternoon. On the roof. Until it got dark and she didn't have enough light.

What was she painting?

Stars of David, same as always. Shadowy, ethereal, twirling among the swirls of colour. Dancing in space, at the whim of her arm movements—twitchy little wrist flicks as she smacked the canvas. And she sketched in a few incomplete Hebrew characters. Fragments of script.

Saba passed her the tubes, helped her mix the colours, choose which characters blended in best with the rest of the painting. Alephs and Yods, dotted all over a plank of wood they used to practise on, and which at the end of the evening Saba brandished at me, proudly declaring that he had finally become a 'man of letters'.

Hurrah, there's the sea!

What a beautiful colour, such a deep blue.

If all goes to plan, we'll get there on time.

On time?

At four o'clock. We're meeting at the entrance to the cemetery. I thought it would be better that way.

I think so too.

I can't remember whether it was from that evening on, or later, that Saba began to suffer from insomnia.

He just couldn't sleep anymore.

When Yaël and I went to bed, he would take up position on the couch in the living room, or on the rocking chair near the window. Sometimes he lit a candle and read for a while, but mostly he stayed shrouded in darkness, without making a sound. He waited until we were asleep and then wandered the streets by himself.

He left around eleven or twelve and came back at dawn. It wasn't until the middle of the day that he dozed off, and only for an hour or two. Sleep deprivation didn't seem to bother him in the slightest. He looked well, radiant. His nocturnal adventures were good for him.

But they caused us a fair amount of worry.

Walking around Tel Aviv had become riskier. At night as well as during the day. The missile attacks had started up again and had escalated in intensity—as a prelude to the peace talks, and to a possible ceasefire.

Without doubt the most hectic time of the whole war must have been that night before the opening session of the peace talks, which were held at the same hotel in Geneva where, three years earlier, Saba had done a reading from one of his collections. An austere, gloomy luxury hotel. As soon as you got through the revolving door, he said, it was blood-curdling: the architecture was stark and the rooms were cavernous. Saba found signing his book in that stuffy environment so excruciating that he couldn't see how anyone would want to sign a peace treaty there.

One evening, I suggested that I accompany him on his 'tour of the city'. He was thrilled. But not surprised. He asked if Yaël knew about it, and if

I had her permission. I said I did, which was not entirely true. Yaël hadn't given me permission to go roaming around with Saba. She had instructed me to.

At first I had refused. If Saba and I copped a missile, she'd end up alone. Stranded all by herself.

What finally persuaded me was when she said she felt awkward around us, as if she was forever coming between us. She wanted to give us time together, so that we'd be more likely to confide in each other. According to her, Saba hadn't yet told me everything: he hadn't outlined everything he wanted to pass on to me.

To us, I corrected her. Saba doesn't have anything to hide from you. He adores you. Your presence animates him as much as mine does.

All the more reason for a private chat, she said. Between you and him.

So I agreed. Still while wondering whether Yaël's request was as spontaneous as it seemed. Or whether, once again, Saba and she were in cahoots.

It was late when we left. Yaël was pretending to be asleep.

I let Saba lead the way. He went down Salame Street, near the warehouses, and turned onto Herzl Street, avoiding the pavements. It was great walking down the middle of the road without having to watch out for traffic, strolling around, zigzagging like two late-night, tipsy party-goers. No chance of getting run over. Not that I recall Saba ever using a pedestrian crossing or waiting for a red light before crossing a street. Road rules were not intended for him. He found them irrelevant. He had the same attitude to his cancer. And to missiles. The conviction that, in order to steer clear of them, you shouldn't give a toss.

He was determined to prove that he had always got away with it. Until now.

At the end of Herzl Street, we turned right onto Ahad Ha'am Street, then left along one of those little lanes that go down to Meir Park.

I waited for Saba to impart his innermost thoughts to me, to shower me with words of wisdom, to recite a speech he had already prepared. But at first he scarcely opened his mouth. As if not to break the silence reigning over the city. A deep silence. A total absence of noise like there is only in the countryside or in the desert. Never in Tel Aviv.

He did tell me one story. The complete silence reminded him of the time when, in the middle of the night, at the centre of the Ramon Crater, he felt he understood or intuited what it meant to be dead. He was walking along the rocky bed of one of the wadis that wind through the bottom of the crater. Alone. All his senses alert. The silence terrified him. The stillness of the air. The indifference of the desert around him, of the firmament above. As if his presence amounted to nothing. As if he were not there. He walked quickly, his shoes pounding the pebbles. But he was dead.

There was no one to see him. No one to hear him. The long nocturnal walk that led nowhere, the feeling of extreme loneliness, true silence, it all sent shivers down his spine. He sensed that on the other side there would be no one he could count on. And that he alone would have to make peace with his soul. But not while he was alive, nor on his death bed. No, it would be immediately afterwards, at the point of coming to an arrangement about eternity.

The best thing to do was to face the facts. As soon as you set foot on the stony ground of oblivion. Play the game. Or at least pretend to, because it was possible to cheat. In fact, it was advisable to, he said. All you had to do was to have a modicum of bad faith: to murmur sweet nothings to yourself, for example. Preferably nonsense, lies. In order to hoodwink loneliness. And infinity too. Which was nothing more than a huge heap of sand and stars. And not nearly as terrifying as one thought, said Saba.

That night in the desert he felt the wings of truth touch his soul. He understood that, on the other side, your only defence was yourself, nothing but your own death—that's what posed a problem to any notion of the absolute, which had no counter-arguments. Saba apprehended all this, and wasn't at all happy about it.

He continued walking until he reached the end of the wadi, and emerged before dawn.

After that story, Saba was silent until we reached Meir Park, at the end of Hasmonean Street. He was a bit short of breath.

We went and sat on a bench, not far from the waterlily pond, which stank of slime and rotting material. It was a clear night, the sky full of stars reflected in the stagnant water. Saba sat with his head bowed, staring at the gravel path, thoughtful, silent.

So then I was the one who spoke—about life and death, about this fucking war, about my brilliant future. I couldn't stop talking.

It did me good.

> OROT RABIN
> Power Station

Rabin's megawatts! It's such bad taste.

Paying homage to the memory of Yitzhak Rabin?

No, associating his name with an ecological pollutant.

When I'd finished spilling my guts, Saba patted me on the back. To console me? To congratulate me? I have no idea. He made no comment on what I had said. He just started up on another subject. Guess what it was?

What?

The story of a book he had borrowed a long time ago from the library on Sheinkin Street, and which he never returned. It seemed to really bug him that he had nicked this book. And yet he'd never taken it back, but treasured it as a reminder of his wrongdoing. As a form of punishment, of penance. By way of atonement, he sentenced himself to read this wonderful book constantly—the book he had prevented the readers in his neighbourhood from discovering.

He was forever rereading it.

You mean Molloy?

Oh, so you know about it?

Does that surprise you?

No...

Well, yes, a bit.

I donated a new copy of it to the library, right after the theft of the other copy.

Saba never mentioned it.

I made it an anonymous donation, and didn't tell him.

```
┌─────────────────────────────┐
│              חל אביב         │
│   54 km      تل ابيب         │
│              Tel Aviv        │
└─────────────────────────────┘
```

On the way back we talked about Grandma. About
her obsessions: how she'd send those typically Jewish
snacks to the kibbutz and we'd chuck them in the
bin. About how she died from cancer after surviving
the Holocaust.

And we talked about you.

Saba told me that, in the eyes of Grandma, you
were like the state of Israel. When you were born,
you brought her hope. You gave her back her faith
in life. But when you grew up, you became moody,
insolent. Grandma had a go at you about it. And

Saba sprang to your defence.

I was perfectly capable of defending myself.

But you didn't.

Against the taunts of a metastasising survivor?

When I was little, I let her tell me off too, even when she was wrong. And cuddle me, even when she started to smell bad. I told Saba.

To defend me?

So that he understood who we were, the next generations. So that he knew how we felt.

That brought a smile to his face.

Being understood is not that important, he said. What matters in life is being accepted for what you are. And doing the same for others. Even when you don't always understand them. Unless they're bad people. Or real idiots. In which case, you're off the hook.

Then we walked on in silence, not a single explosion to interrupt our stroll. Perhaps the enemy had run out of ammunition. Or the negotiations in the ugly hotel in Geneva were progressing after all. When we got back, Yaël was still asleep. We waited for her to wake up so we could have breakfast with her. And begin a new day of filming.

INTERIOR OF THE GREAT SYNAGOGUE
OF TEL AVIV (ALLENBY STREET)

1.

Saba stands on the platform of the pulpit. He is wearing a prayer shawl. He is rocking back and forth, muttering passionately.

The camera pans to the big stained-glass window. The image is blurred by the glare from the outside light.

The image comes into focus gradually. A winged being appears in the field of vision.

Yaël, dressed up as an angel, is leaning over the mezzanine reserved for women. She pretends to take flight. Flaps her wings.

Saba raises his head (without appearing surprised).

2.

The angel has joined the man at the pulpit.

The angel takes his hand and leads him towards the front of the synagogue.

They climb the steps to the Torah ark, where the Scrolls of the Law are kept.

The angel pulls open the velvet curtain in front of the cabinet housing the sacred parchments.

Saba lets go of the angel's hand. He opens the cabinet door and steps inside. He disappears (giving the impression that he has passed over to the other side, into another world or another dimension).

The sound of celestial trumpets can be heard echoing in the distance...

That's when the air-raid siren went off, Mum. You wouldn't believe your eyes. Or your ears. Wait till I show you the clip. The sirens began to wail at exactly the second Saba stepped into the cabinet.

Exactly where it says 'celestial trumpets' in my script.

Yaël was brilliant. Standing there alone, facing out onto the huge empty hall. I kept filming her for a bit. Then, as there was nowhere else to shelter, I dashed for the holy ark, yelling at Yaël to crawl in quickly next to Saba.

I could see he was already reaching for her, his arm draped in white satin and tassels. He hadn't had time to take off the prayer shawl.

I leaped up to the top of the steps and pushed Yaël inside the cupboard. Her wings got in the way; they stuck out too far.

We had to rip them off her.

Once the wings were off, Yaël clutched her back as if we had hurt her.

Saba pushed her to the rear of the holy ark and I pulled the door shut on us.

The first blasts came only a few seconds later. The missiles were probably fired from nearby. Long-range missiles take longer to arrive. And the sound of them is much worse.

We stayed huddled in the dark until things calmed down. We weren't frightened of what was happening outside.

We were on the other side.

When we stepped out of the ark it was still light, but I didn't feel like filming anymore. Neither did Yaël. Saba had to reconcile himself to not continuing with the shoot. He just asked me to wait for a few minutes. He climbed back up to the pulpit, still wrapped in the big white shawl. And he prayed.

I recognised the psalms he recited. He launched

into the liturgy in a clear voice. He chanted each word, each verse, without stammering. He who never stepped inside a synagogue.

He had learnt it all when he was a child.

And never forgotten any of it.

Your dad also knows the Psalms of David.

Yes, he remembers them from school. Me too. But Saba learned them at home. From his grandfather.

Not at school.

The Hefer Valley Regional Council welcomes you

Yaël's parents told me that they didn't know a single hymn. Under threat of imprisonment, it was forbidden by the Soviets to learn them, or even to speak Hebrew. That's why they fled as soon as they could, why they left everything to come to Israel. So there you go, after all that, they still don't go to synagogue, and can't speak Hebrew. And now they live in Los Angeles.

They tried to come back at the beginning of the war, because Yaël refused to leave while she still could, to join them over there in the US. Then there were no more flights in either direction. They only started up again two or three days ago. The occasional flight. Her parents jumped on the first plane.

They're here, you know. They arrived the day before yesterday.

They don't want to see me.

> **Mikhmoret**
> (RESTAURANT, BEACH)

You can smoke if you want. Don't worry about me.

Did you hear me, Mum?

I'm lost for words, Naor. Words to make you feel better. Words from before.

You don't have to say them. A mother's words are like a psalm. You don't forget them.

That's sweet of you.

Do you still smoke Noblesse? I can't believe those disgusting cigarettes still exist. Incredible!

Before we left the synagogue, Saba took off the prayer shawl. It was as if he too was removing his wings. He turned towards us, slightly embarrassed that we had seen him praying.

And because, after all, the whole thing was his fault.

Outside, as we set off, I took hold of Yaël's hand

and apologised for pushing her into the ark. She didn't seem to hear me.

We walked without speaking for a long time. Saba trotted in front. He wanted to leave us in peace.

We headed straight back to Florentin, to Yoni's. Not because we feared another attack, but because we weren't in the mood for walking. The city looked trashed: the wind was stirring up the rubbish that had accumulated almost everywhere. Dead creepers hung from balconies like burnt tinsel. The flowers had withered in the window boxes. On Rothschild Boulevard, the lawns had turned yellow. So, with nothing to graze on, the gazelles had left.

Only the bougainvilleas had held up.

And it was too quiet—like a sleepy Saturday morning, so still you'd end up catatonic. A never-ending Saturday morning.

Tel Aviv without people. Without nightlife. Without noise.

In the end, it's a stupid third-world city, badly laid-out and not very clean. Not much bigger than Quito. As stifling as Guayaquil. I don't know why I'm talking about Ecuador. Perhaps because of the indigenous people there, the range of different groups. Hasidics, gays, Arabs, urban folk, lost souls, the tattooed, the pierced, the circumcised, male or female, wearing a kippah, or a veil, their paths all crossing there, all crowded together. Perhaps because it's a city that is both chaotic and happy. Like the cities you find at the foot of the Andes or on the banks of the Amazon, rather than on the edge of the desert. A city that seems to go out of its way not to be beautiful. So that you become attached to the people who live there, not to its bricks and mortar.

We were pleased to be back in Florentin. Where there is nothing to see. Nothing to miss. Where art and peace are hardwired into the place. Where the future is playing out in warehouses. Where the word 'failure' has no meaning. An alternative neighbourhood like any other. Almost. Where the hippies are, for the most part, former commandos.

From time to time, Saba turned around to look at us. Especially when we passed places where we used to hang out. Cafés mostly. And the cinémathèque, its glass walls covered by soot from the explosions. But not broken. He suggested we break down the door of a pub in Lilienblum Street to have a beer, and cheer ourselves up.

Yaël told him that was enough nonsense for today. He was thrilled to be told off by her. It meant he was forgiven. He set off again at a much livelier pace. Still out front, checking all the nooks and crannies of the city as if he were a council inspector.

Deep down, Saba wasn't unhappy about what was happening to Tel Aviv. He told me as much one night when we were on the roof at Yoni's, looking at the sunset. He said it did no one any harm to get a kick up the arse from time to time. And that we Israelis badly needed it. Because we had got stuck in a stalemate. Not only with the Palestinians, which was of course unfortunate. But also and especially with ourselves, which was much worse.

So the evacuation was timely. It gave us an undreamt-of chance to wipe the slate clean. To start again. In his mind, Zionism as an idea was not a failure. But it was stagnant. It had come unstuck in its application. Because of this and that. Those were his exact words. This and that. He spoke about restating our attempts at Jewish socialism. About the importance of education. 'Everything stems from that.' And about being kinder in general. To poor people, and to Arabs.

He finished up saying optimistically that the post-war period would be a prosperous time.

מבואות ים
Mevo'ot Yam
Youth Village

There's a Sea-Turtle Rescue Centre there, just down the road. Next to the village with the reintegration program for disadvantaged adolescents.

I was glad Yaël had finally spoken, and reprimanded me too. She made me promise never, ever again to throw her into a shelter or a hideout. And she decreed an outright boycott on air-raid sirens. Never again were we going to let sirens disturb our peace. Or missiles interrupt our film-making.

From now on, we were going to behave as if there was no war.

As if the war had never happened.

Do you think the turtles know? That they have to come here to be rescued?

נתניה
נتانيا
5 km
Netanya

It was at that moment, while she was issuing me with more instructions, that I noticed she was still wearing the braces to which she had attached her angel wings. Rather large braces, almost clownish— the ones she'd dug up from Yoni's wardrobe.

I felt jealous: Yaël wearing another guy's clothes, as if there was something going on between them. Behind my back. Jealous that this guy was giving his place to her, his bedroom, his bed. As if he was keeping watch over her, from afar.

It's how we all felt, living at Yoni's.

That, from wherever he was, he was keeping us safe. From the bottom of a trench, or from the top of a hill.

By shooting at those who meant to harm us.

Between them and us, there was only him. A fairly quiet guy, not very chatty. A guy with an army helmet, a familiar face. We used to have late-night drinks with him. I had revised with him for the end-of-semester exam on the films of Cecil B., and I'd watched a whole season of *Game of Thrones* with him.

Yoni also protected us in another way. His apartment enfolded us as if we were in a cocoon. We were at home there. Old-style, sparsely furnished, it was a perfect fit with the state of mind we were in. There was nothing but the essentials. Lots of formica, in bright colours, yellows and greens, from the sixties. Appliances to match. An enamel gas stove. A stainless-steel toaster. An Arabic coffee pot with a wooden handle on the side. A round copper tray with six white porcelain cups, all chipped. Even the living-room ceiling fan was vintage. The brand was Star, with Bakelite blades.

Everywhere, the decor was simple, modest, plain. As if anything too beautiful was indecent. There was an old black-and-white photo of Tel Aviv in the 1920s, where you could see the dunes at the end of a boulevard crowded with horse-drawn carriages, Arab handcarts loaded with fruit and vegetables, open-roofed motor cars, and fashionable people with umbrellas. A framed poster of a Raffi Lavie exhibition at the Gordon Gallery. Empty bottles on a shelf. Johnnie Walker, Elite Arak, Stoli. Bedouin rugs of woven wool, to hide the cracks in the tiled floor. In short, skillfully presented austerity. Socially correct, you might say. Verging on virtuous.

Which is in perfect keeping with the person. Because Yoni is actually like that. The total cliché. Like Dad, in fact. Just as conventional. But in reverse.

Yoni is pretty relaxed. Never ashamed to take it easy, not give a damn about whatever. All the same, he's not at all disenchanted. Not at all the back-to-nature type so revered by Dad, the 'kibbutznik' with completely fixed ideas about pioneering, about the Labour movement, always reeling off his set of utopian dreams—the failure of which he admits with an element of pride, as well as an ill-disguised bitterness.

You're so determined to imitate your grandfather, to speak like him, like a cynic. To think, like him, that you have to be different, original at any price. That you have to stand alone.

I study cinema, Mum. So I can make films. Films that are different. Standalones.

Wanting to distinguish yourself from others, to take the high moral ground. There's nothing more banal.

Unless you get it right.

Do you think Saba got it right?

You know I don't.

And what about you?

Likewise! What about you? Weren't you ever tempted to behave like Saba? All those eccentric performances.

Of course I was. When I was your age. More to please him than for myself.

I don't see what the difference is.

Excuse me?

Between getting personal gratification and giving someone else pleasure.

Even now?

It's easy to be analytical and level accusations—after the fact.

You know perfectly well that's not what I meant.

We've had a lot of misunderstandings, you and I. Don't you think so?

The ashtray is there. Yes, the little drawer under the radio.

Are you angry?

Annoyed.

It bothers me that you might be right, after all. And that Saba might be wrong.

> **ROADWORKS**
> Reduced speed for 3km

When we got back to the apartment, we opened tins of tuna and vegetables, and a packet of biscuits that was past its use-by date. We had stomach cramps from being so scared. And we'd worked up an appetite on our walk across town. We settled in on the living-room couch. I put a spare battery in my phone and we viewed the day's filming while we ate.

Saba looked older on film. Hunched over, wrapped in white wool. The pale material highlighted his dark colouring, the deep furrows of his wrinkles. It was the first time that I noticed just how oriental he looked. And it was also the first time that I pictured him as a child, running among the benches in the Baghdad synagogue. While his father and his uncles prayed, wrapped in their huge shawls, wearing their gold-braided skullcaps. I saw them through his eyes. Very clearly. People from another time. Another place.

I've always had trouble getting my head around the idea that I am part Iraqi. Whereas the Slavic side that comes to me via Dad, and Grandma too, seems completely normal. I feel like I've lost all the splendour that accompanies my lineage, all that Sephardic magnificence. For me, Saba was one of the few remaining guardians of all that. Perhaps the very last custodian.

You'll see, in the final shot, when he disappears into the ark, and passes to the 'other side', there's a whole world that vanishes with him. Not just a man. It'll have the same impact on you, when I show you the scene. And you'll hear the sirens wailing.

During the viewing, Saba didn't touch his food. He relived each moment, shot by shot. He told us that, as he stepped over the threshold of the holy cabinet, he genuinely had the feeling of going to the other side, as he plunged in among the Torah scrolls stored there in caskets, like mummies in their sarcophagi. He had been struck by 'how bright the darkness was'. Those were his words. And he also said that he would never have imagined the dying of the light to be so dazzling.

'Nor so deafening,' added Yaël. Our eardrums were still vibrating from the roar of the sirens.

We laughed. And Saba stuck his fork in the pink and oily tuna flesh. He was starving.

Like anyone who has just been resurrected.

To Netanya via the coast

I haven't watched that scene since then. Did I tell
you that?

Yes.

And Saba has made no further mention of dying
at all.

After that strange day, we cast ourselves adrift for good. We lost our bearings, and lived in the moment, as they say. In benign indifference. Which was not difficult. Tel Aviv thrives exclusively on the present moment. Tomorrow has always been uncertain. And that's just fine. That nothing is certain. That everything is up for grabs. Even your right to exist.

Uncertainty is a source of joy. It frees you up.

Nothing is guaranteed. You are not owed anything. Your Holy Temple will be burned down, your Land pillaged—in order to liberate you from any tranquillity of mind, and to remove the trappings of all things certain.

From that day on, Yaël decided she wouldn't be frightened of missiles anymore. And Saba decided he would no longer live in such dread of his imminent death. As for me, I couldn't come up with something not to be frightened of. Actually, I didn't really try. I'm truly sorry I didn't.

It wouldn't have made any difference, my darling.

At the time, all I felt was Yaël's determination, Saba's joie de vivre. And an indescribable lightness in my soul. Which I had always had, even before, without realising it.

I knew then that it was from in there, from within my soul, that Yaël drew her courage, and Saba the last vestiges of his strength.

Because I was Tel Aviv.

I was their city.

A city they had inhabited with their dreams, their fears. A city in the heart of which they could walk around and forget their loneliness. A welcoming city, a party city, as the tourism office is forever trumpeting. I set the mood for them, an environment ripe for them to express their love. I was the crowd, the audience.

I didn't realise it until that night. I was amazed they relied on me like that. Me? Nice guy. Not very serious. Not even good-looking. Rather lazy.

Like Tel Aviv.

Where indifference is seen as courage.

Where indolence makes you strong.

```
נתניה
نتانيا
Netanya
(TO THE CITY CENTRE)
```

Another place where life is good. According to the tourism office.

And a lot cheaper than Tel Aviv.

And less humid, what's more.

The authorities have estimated that approximately twenty-five thousand people remained in the city after the evacuation and the round-ups.

Is that all?

That's the official figure.

We never saw the others. Almost never. No doubt they were playing it safe, watching their step. They didn't waver like us. Because we never saw them, we ended up feeling that we were the only ones. Separate. Outside the rest of the world.

We only witnessed one arrest. In the middle of the street. A couple in their fifties. They didn't try to resist the police. They were probably tired of being dirty and eating badly. They climbed into the police van obediently; they looked sad. We watched the scene from a porch where we'd been hiding, and didn't show much interest, or compassion. As if what was happening there, beneath our noses, was of no concern to us.

Not our business.

I almost got arrested too. By myself. Like an idiot.

Saba and Yaël wanted to do something nice for me, so they helped me carry my windsurfer to the sea—balanced on a wheelbarrow that we dug up from a building site. We wobbled the whole thing down to Banana Beach.

As soon as I got a short distance out from the coast, it was heaven. I forgot everything. The evacuation, the patrols, the drones. The confines of Yoni's cramped apartment.

I'd made trips outside in all weather, even in the rain, and at night. But never alone on the expanse of the sea. Completely alone under the blue sky.

A breeze from the north-west, about twelve knots. Forty centimetres of swell. And no one. No one on the beach, or on the water. No one, as far as the eye could see.

I was already too far away to make out Saba and Yaël. All I could see was the silhouette of the city, like a frieze, outlined against the blue.

And then in the depths of the silence, in the middle of the sea, I heard the blades of a helicopter whacking against the wind. Louder and louder. Like in a film about the Vietnam War, like in Oliver Stone's *Platoon*.

I watched its shadow ripple over the waves, then looked up and realised it was heading straight for me. An air-force chopper. Huge, heavy, painted green.

It circled above me three times. Symmetrical orbits, like a seagull. And then it banked, lining me up with the axis of its rotor blades. Instantly, I was in the grips of the downdraft. My board was whipped up several metres in the air. My sail tore. And I was flung away, tumbling head over heels.

Still tilting towards me, the helicopter lost altitude. The door of the cabin opened and a guy in an aviator suit appeared. His face was concealed by the perspex visor of his helmet. Headphones bulged on the sides. At first I thought he was going to throw down a rope ladder and order me to climb on board. But he made no move. I guessed he was checking me out. I raised my thumb to show him I was okay, that I wasn't injured. He replied with an obscene gesture, sticking his middle finger up at me. And the helicopter rose back up into the sky.

The pilots were annoyed at seeing a guy windsurfing, while not far away the combat was in full swing. I suppose they thought it was indecent that I was enjoying my life while so many others were losing theirs. Mostly young people my age. Who also liked the beach, and surfing.

But I didn't think I was showing disrespect to Yoni by hopping on my board. Nor was I was betraying the soldiers. On the contrary, I was presenting them with a form of revenge.

I wasn't aware that the slaughter they were involved in required us to pay homage. I apologise for that.

I should have had a more deferential attitude to the war.

חל אביב
31 km   تل ابيب
Tel Aviv

Dad almost came to get you. We were worried sick.
Yaël's parents too. They called us several times. But we
didn't have any news.

We would have needed a carrier pigeon to get
news to you.

Saba was happy to suggest that we tie messages
to balloons and let them loose on windy days. And
Yaël's idea was to write messages on the roofs. With
spray paint. But if we revealed our presence we
would run the risk of becoming a target.

We were worried too. About you. And we had

no idea how the fighting was going. But, hey, things are never that clear around here. Even when there's no war.

When there's no war?

Military war, Mum.

You know perfectly well what I mean.

It was hard being cut off from everything. We felt as if we didn't exist, as if we were living in zero-gravity atmosphere, like astronauts on a space station. But without a miniature Earth visible through the porthole.

I wonder if dragging the windsurfer right through the city, to the sea, was not somehow our way of making sure we got arrested. Like that couple we'd seen, who were fed up with hiding, and with looking over their shoulder the whole time.

On more than one occasion, we talked about throwing in the towel, about giving ourselves up to the authorities. To tell you the truth, it was tempting. Saba made it clear that he would not have objected. It was Yaël who didn't want to.

We took a vote on it. I was in favour. Yaël was against. Saba abstained. With a ballot like that, we were not likely to be leaving the space station anytime soon.

Dad made a big mistake not coming to get us.

Do you hold it against him?

If it had been me, I wouldn't have thought twice about it. Not for a minute.

Saba shouldn't have abstained, that's all!

And I shouldn't have let myself go along with the stupid vote. Which does not let Dad off the hook in the slightest.

As for Saba, I'll let you guess what he's feeling. He'll tell you himself. I told him to wait for us in front of the cemetery gate. At around four o'clock.

Yaël is buried in Avenue 5. Right near the entrance.

It was still light. Saba was walking ahead.

We had just left the painter Reuven Rubin's house, which the council had turned into a museum. Yaël wanted to see the paintings on exhibit there. Galilean landscapes, the Jerusalem Hills, Tel Aviv port. Portraits of pre-war actresses of Zionist bohemia. Most of the canvases were rather primitive in style. Naïve. Too optimistic. Lacking that spark of genius. But you can't go past them, Yaël told us: they were the beginnings of a truly Israeli painting tradition. Especially when it came to colour.

It was the colours that Yaël was keen to see—on the canvases, but also on the palettes and sketchbooks kept in the studio, which had been reconstructed as if Reuven Rubin had just walked out a moment ago to get a coffee or a snack and was going to come back.

We had got up early that morning, intending to film a scene in the gallery.

The route we took from Yoni's place to the museum, from Florentin to Bialik Street, was the perfect pilgrims' way. Saba was keen to walk past the building where he had lived with Grandma. And where you were born. He showed Yaël the back courtyard, with the old stunted palm tree, still lopsided, still standing; the aloe-vera plants; the rubbish. The Vespa carcass was still there, the one you used to climb onto and straddle when you were little, now covered in brambles.

Yaël led us to the house of her dreams, at the top of Montefiore Street. A grand building in the shape of an Elizabethan theatre. You know which one I mean?

Yes, of course. With balconies like loges.

That's the one.

Next, I dragged Saba and Yaël down Lilienblum Street to the only shop in Israel where I could stock up on 8-millimetre film for my Eumig camera with the electric motor. You wind it up with a key, like an old-fashioned clock.

That's the camera I should have used to make our film. I still had unused rolls of film.

I stared through the filthy window frame at the mess of editing equipment, antiquated record players, an old typewriter, and I had the feeling that an era was coming to an end. That I was there in order to draw a line under a period of my life. Was that a premonition?

After the evacuation, nothing would be the same anymore. Tel Aviv would not be the same: no longer immune, no longer exempted from History and Geography classes. From now on, the city would have a past. Just like Paris or Madrid. A memorable past, and wrinkles.

Wandering the streets that day, all three of us felt a sort of premature nostalgia, I think. It was as if we were walking through an outdated, abandoned theatre set that we could not resign ourselves to leave.

Wasn't that why we had refused to evacuate? So as not to let ourselves be catapulted towards the future. Towards the days to come, which Saba liked to predict would be no less idiotic than ours. And which Yaël dreaded, because canvases a lot more sophisticated than those of Reuven Rubin would be produced—churned out on a printer.

I proposed that the future would also bring peace, one day. That gave them a laugh.

It was worth a try.

During the walk, I realised just how attached Yaël was to Tel Aviv. Not in the same way Saba and I were. In a much deeper, more intimate way, almost secret.

She didn't pour her heart out about her passion for the city. Not like Saba did, for everything he saw and everything that happened: the colourful night-life, the cafés, the fun. The young people he loved and missed—for him, Yaël was their muse.

She didn't delight in the city the way I did either, as an opportunist, a pleasure-seeker. Every inch of my body revelled in the place. I let it permeate me, pulse through my limbs, run through my veins. I was one of those people who breathes in time with the city's heartbeat.

People who don't understand Tel Aviv, or who don't like it, describe the city as a bubble. A bubble hermetically sealed, floating in the air, divorced from reality. And from the rest of Israel.

Yaël lived curled up inside that bubble. She wasn't interested in the rest of the country, apart from the desert. And she couldn't care less about reality. She was an artist. Like Reuven Rubin. Or Marcel Janco. A lover of Israel, of its pictures, of its Bible, of its lovers. Like Chagall, who would have painted her as a Jewish bride gliding like the moon above the roofs.

In her bright bubble.

Not far to go now.

The traffic's building up.

If I'd insisted, Saba would have come around to
the idea of giving up. The air raid that struck while
we were filming in the Grand Synagogue had given
him pause. He preferred to bow out on a high note,
not pulverised by a missile.

As for me, honestly, I no longer understood the
point of persevering, of resisting.

What exactly was the purpose of this obstinacy? To piss off the Arabs?

To annoy the world?

Ultimately, Yaël was the only one who knew what we were doing there. Not Saba, who was preparing for a much more definitive evacuation. Not me—I had only stayed because of him; at least, that's what I told myself.

After Yaël died, Saba admitted to me that they had indeed been in cahoots, the pair of them. That the whole thing had been a set-up. He wasn't the one who had decided to spend his last days in the abandoned city, like some eccentric old man acting on a mystic impulse, or on a mere whim. It was Yaël who, despite the danger, had insisted. She had begged Saba to help her.

She had no desire at all to go to your place, to the kibbutz. Or anywhere else. But she knew that I wouldn't listen to her. Her parents held me responsible for her safety. And I thought it was my duty to protect her.

But Tel Aviv was the only place Yaël felt safe. From those at war with us. From those who have morality and justice on their side. From the ants in Aesop's fable, who, when the cold wind arrives, tell the hungry cicada to sing the winter away.

Tel Aviv was a sanctuary for her. Where even God was welcome. Saba, who was in complete agreement on this, went further, telling her that Tel Aviv was like the cities of refuge mentioned in the Bible. There were six at the time.

Three on the other side of the Jordan River. And three on this side, in Canaan. Six Tel Avivs!

When the sirens went off, Yaël reached for my hand, pulling it in front of us a bit, so we would continue walking, and not seek shelter.

Saba turned round to check on us. He saw what was going on and stepped up his pace. That made us laugh, because he started to trot, as if he was late for a meeting, or some job he had to do.

Yaël walked with her head held high, staring straight in front of her. I couldn't tell if she was proud of how gutsy she was, or scared stiff.

The sirens continued for a while, but there were no missiles whistling above, no explosions. The sky was empty, and bright blue.

It was only when we entered the Nachlat Binyamin pedestrian area, at the point where it intersects with Ramban Street, that we heard a blast and saw a vapour trail rise in the air and turn into a little round cloud, like we had seen dozens of times—the blazing head of a rocket intercepted in full flight.

Yaël was still holding my hand. A few seconds later, I felt her grip tighten and then she let go. As if she had tripped on something. I tried to catch her, to pull her towards me.

She collapsed. Slowly. Her hand still in mine. And a piece of metal stuck in her head. A small uneven triangle, with serrated edges. The point was buried among her dark curls like a comb in a flamenco dancer's bun.

The metal was still smoking and I could smell her scorched hair and skin.

I stood still as a liquid current ran through my body.

It was still light. Saba was walking ahead. He didn't see what happened. Or hear anything: the metal shard had ripped through the air in silence, and Yaël hadn't uttered a sound.

Do you want to stop on the side of the road and have a bit of a rest?

No, he's waiting for us.

He's waiting for you.

I don't know how long I stayed there. With her hand in mine. She was leaning backwards, her fall halted by my arm as I held her. Her head didn't hit the ground. Her eyes stayed open.

I felt a tap on my shoulder and thought my name was being called. *Naor, Naor…* Saba's face appeared in my vision, his eyes fixed on mine. He grabbed hold of me, tugged at me, shook me. Yaël's body fell to the ground.

Saba closed her eyelids. I quickly took her back into my arms again. We headed to the Reading emergency-services centre, in the opposite direction, north. It was the only one we knew of.

Saba no longer walked ahead. He accompanied

me in silence. As if he was frightened of breaking my train of thought, upsetting me.

We turned left into the main aisle of the Carmel Market, where we'd been on our first night. When we were fugitives. Rebels. When the rats had gone to hide in the sewers, and when the InterContinental Hotel had collapsed before our eyes. Then we went along by the sea to the Yarkon estuary and the bridge.

There was no one there when I entered the courtyard of the emergency-services centre. With Yaël in my arms. I called out for help.

They emerged, one by one, their personal protective-equipment kits slung over their shoulders. And guns, which looked like 9-millimetre pistols.

One of them offered me a drink bottle.

It was Saba who explained to them how the tragedy had happened. Listening to him, I felt like such an idiot. I could tell from his quavering voice that he felt like an idiot too. To have believed that he was smarter than the missiles.

To have diced with death. But not his own.

The instructions were clear enough. In case of attack, run to the nearest covered area, if you can reach it within twenty seconds. Hunker down there until ten minutes after the sirens have stopped roaring. Otherwise, lie on the ground anywhere, your hands over your head. You didn't have to be a genius to get it right, for God's sake.

But, you see, Yaël didn't want to lie down in the gutter. She didn't want to surrender to the war.

I watched the emergency-services workers take her body away. I hadn't noticed them lifting her out of my arms. They went into a shed; Saba followed.

A nurse made me take some pills.

Later, a military chaplain came to see me. An air-force rabbi from the nearby base at Sde Dov airport, where the anti-aircraft batteries that defended Tel Aviv were kept. He prayed. Instead of me.

The pills had knocked me out.

הרצליה
5 km   هرتسليا
Herzliya

I didn't see Saba until the next day. He kept vigil over the body.

```
┌─────────────────────────────┐
│              חל אביב         │
│   12 km      تل ابيب         │
│              Tel Aviv        │
└─────────────────────────────┘
```

With the emergency-services workers, the military rabbi, Saba and me, there were the requisite ten men to say the prayer for the dead. I recited it.

The rabbi passed me a prayer book, but I didn't even glance at it. The words came to me instinctively; I didn't have to think about them. I uttered them without the slightest conviction, my soul filled with bitterness.

The rabbi had contacted Yaël's parents overnight and obtained their permission to bury her, after explaining that Jewish law stipulates the dead must be buried as quickly as possible, out of respect for the cadaver.

He sent them a photo, via WhatsApp, of Yaël: cleaned up, hair combed, laid out on a stretcher.

I also know he spoke to Dad on the phone that night, on the landline. It was Saba's idea, because he couldn't bring himself to talk to you.

And neither could I.

The rabbi was very kind on the phone, very decent.

Yes, he has a gentle voice. His gestures are calm and collected. And his facial expressions are soothing. He was the one who advised me to go and get you as soon as the roads were open, to drive you to Tel Aviv to meet up with Saba, and for you to make peace with each other.

No one dragged us off to the police station after Yaël's funeral. The peace negotiations had begun over there in Geneva. There was no point in arresting us and arranging for us to be shipped off somewhere when the evacuation order was about to be lifted from one day to the next.

As soon as the formalities were over, Saba and I returned to Florentin.

Saba is wearing his beige suit and Panama hat. He is standing with his back to the French doors, facing the easel.

Yaël is sitting on a stool, in the middle of the room. She sits there without moving for a few moments, then reaches her arm out towards the painter, inviting him to come over to her.

He refuses.

The model keeps her arm out.

Saba leans towards the canvas and starts work. He's nervous. He mixes some paints, shakes a few brushes, and every now and again picks up a stained cloth.

When he raises his head and turns towards the centre of the room again, Yaël is no longer there. He stares around, but doesn't see that she is standing behind him. Nor does he see the slender shadow cast by the sunlight onto the carpet next to his own shadow, caught fleetingly by the camera, as if by accident.

The camera moves back and forth between the figures and their shadows on the carpet. The figures remain motionless, while their shadows move and intermingle to form only a single shadow, which lengthens as the sun drops down.

(Try to capture the gradual dimming of tones and colours.)

The shadow reaches an arm out to the painter.

But the painter turns back to the easel. (Camera movement follows his gaze.)

Shot of the painting on the easel. Full screen.

What is the painting of? To be decided

(Suggestions: a portrait without a face. Or anything unfinished. A scene filmed as if the canvas were a screen. The words THE END.)

I really thought that was going to be the end of Saba. But he held it together. He hung on. Out of decency, I think. Or else out of bitterness. Because Yaël had jumped the gun on him, by going first.

And he also knew you were going to come.

To tell him off? Pardon him? Listen to him?

To make peace with him, perhaps.

He was the one who wanted the three of us to meet in front of Yaël's grave. He whispered it to me in the middle of the burial, while they were shovelling earth onto the body.

After the service, while we were walking back up the cemetery aisle, I remembered the walk in the desert he had told me about before we sat on the bench in Meir Park. And I imagined Yaël striding along the bed of a huge wadi that led to the end of infinity, or of nowhere. How would she go about making a deal with eternity?

Would she use her charm? Her cheek? Or would she cheat, as Saba had advised her to do?

She was alone, in the depths of the long night. Completely alone. But, essentially, no more than we were, Saba and I, the ones she had ditched. We felt like orphans. And so did Tel Aviv.

While she was there, with us, Tel Aviv was full of life. Now it was at a standstill, deserted. Hardly worth using as a film location. The vacuum Yaël left behind her extended to the whole city and robbed it of its soul.

And us—we were like the streets of Tel Aviv, neglected, abandoned, filled with absence.

So we decided to get back to shooting *Evacuation*, to finishing the film. In homage to Yaël, and as a way of warding off the curse that her death had put on the city.

You understand: Tel Aviv was falling apart. We absolutely had to do something about it.

```
┌─────────────────────────┐
│              חל אביב      │
│   12 km      تل ابيب      │
│              Tel Aviv     │
└─────────────────────────┘
```

We took up where we had left off.

You remember?

The point where the painter is leaning towards his canvas, while his shadow intermingles with the shadow of death, who, disguised as an artist's model, has come to get him in his studio.

In the original script, it's not clear whether he is going to follow the model.

To tell the truth, we hadn't decided. Saba had been practising in front of the mirror: grimacing as if he were at death's door, and falling to the ground like a deadweight. But, despite his insistence, I was loath to film him giving up the ghost. Because the character he was playing could just as easily refuse his destiny as submit to it.

We discussed it at length, hesitating, weighing up the pros and cons, umming and ahhing.

Then, in the meantime, it wasn't him, but someone else whom death took away.

Our actresss!

And our only audience.

Yaël had the key role, around which everything else revolved.

I had written the script of *Evacuation* for her, just like Cecil B had written the role of Cleopatra for Claudette Colbert. He had constructed pyramids, erected sphinxes to the glory of his queen. A queen of cinema.

Not of Egypt.

And, for my queen, I too had built a magical realm. And her dream city.

In the end, wasn't Tel Aviv just that? A location, a decor. A pretext?

A cardboard city. Illusory. An illusion. A figment.

Nothing more than an agglomeration.

Of all our hopes.

I couldn't tell you how many days we stayed locked up in Yoni's apartment, moping around, mulling things over. But when I told Saba what I'd been thinking, what I've just told you, he leaped up, grabbed me by the arm and dragged me outside.

To go and see if Tel Aviv existed. Those were his words.

He was angry.

Hurtling down the stairs behind him, I decided it wasn't that bad, after all, to go and see what was happening out there. Find some inspiration. Have a look around.

Get a breath of fresh air.

Yes, I suppose so.

We headed down to the beach, where a light wind was blowing, and walked quietly along the boardwalk all the way to Jaffa. And then back up to the old city to do the rounds of the places where I used to hang out with Yaël.

Can you believe that not one of them had been hit during the air raids—not one!

It was awful.

On Dizengoff Street, where it intersects with Gordon Street, the Italian restaurant on the corner was intact. The beige canvas awnings were untouched, as were the chemist opposite and the adjoining art gallery, their shop windows almost spotless.

As if nothing had happened.

I felt like smashing the gallery shopfront, kicking it in, or throwing stones. Saba restrained me. He said that the death of someone doesn't change anything. Or not much. And that it was better that way.

He spoke about those who had died already in this war, about those who had died in the wars before this one. And how nothing in the slightest had changed as a result.

And that calmed you down?

This is where we turn off. To the cemetery.

I haven't been back since Yaël's burial, you know.

You don't need to look so distant, Mum.

I hope you're not reacting to Saba's rant about the war, and about death.

I really hope not.

No, that's not it, Naor. You have to understand: I'm a bit stressed anyway.

Because you're going to see Saba again?

And this city.

Which you should never have left.

Which I miss sometimes.

We kept walking, up to Ben Yehuda Street, where we ran into the first cars coming back into the city. Re-entering with little flags stuck on their antennae and wing mirrors, pennants flapping like crazy in the wind, so you could barely make out the blue stars and stripes, the Israeli flags.

As if they were whited out.

I stood there on the pavement for ages, transfixed by the manic fluttering wings, like feverish fruit bats flitting among the trees on Allenby Street.

The emblem of our nation kept flapping in the air, but I couldn't make out the flag itself.

It was hazy, imprecise.

As wavy and blurry as if Yaël had painted it.

As if it were returning the favour, congratulating her.

I recalled the final shot we had filmed, when the painter is studying the canvas on his easel. We hadn't established whether it would be a finished painting or just a few brushstrokes. Or whether it would serve as a screen on which we would project moving images.

I snapped out of my daze and, without checking with Saba, who had gone to sit on a bench, grabbed my phone and started filming the procession of cars. I zoomed in on the blue-and-white flags flapping against the sides of the vehicles. I envisaged exactly what the effect would be: one of Yaël's paintings projected onto the artist's canvas, then a dissolve into these images of the return to Tel Aviv, of life starting up again.

I knew exactly which of Yaël's compositions to use, the very last one, which she had painted on the roof at Yoni's.

The one where she had smudged the outlines of the Stars of David with a rag, so they floated in space, lost in the brush swirls, swept up by the burst of colours.

I headed straight over and sat on the bench with Saba, to show him the sequence I had just filmed, and to ask him what he thought of my idea. He thought it was lovely. That's all he had to say— lovely!

Oh, and also that he wasn't a fan of dissolve shots. I didn't persist.

On the way back, we went down Rothschild Boulevard. It was still peaceful, apart from the occasional car going past. We walked slowly, as if we were out on a casual stroll between the rows of trees along the central path.

Saba was lost in thought. Something was bothering him. It was obvious.

'And the painter, what happened to him?' he asked out of the blue.

I was about to reply when we both suddenly jumped sideways at the same time. A sprinkler had sprayed us with water.

Then another one.

There was nowhere to take shelter. Jets of water like fencing swords were crisscrossing the whole pathway. The boulevard was covered in a fine cloud of droplets.

We were drenched—in cool water that revived our bodies.

All at once, the sprinkler system had started up.

After all that time.

Saba buttoned up his dripping Hemingway jacket. I rolled up the hems of my jeans. And we weaved our way between the sprinklers. Capering along to the *click-clack* rhythm they made as they turned.

תל אביב - יפו
ي فا-تل آبيب
Tel Aviv–Jaffa

Look, Saba's already there.

I'm going to park a bit further up, in the shade.

Should I drop you here?

AUTHOR'S NOTE

This novel was written in Tel Aviv, sitting outside the café A Consolation and a Half, not far from Rothschild Boulevard.

My gratitude goes to Myriam Anderson, my editor, for having made this book possible, and for accompanying me in the writing process.

My gratitude also goes to Penny Hueston for her marvellous translation of this text, as well as for her enthusiasm and support.

Yaël's paintings are inspired by *Abstract Ivri*: www.facebook.com/abstractivri.